W9-BPY-764

THE
SNOWY
DAY

EZRA JACK KEATS

THE
SNOWY
DAY

xz
K

New York · The Viking Press

VIKING
Published by Penguin Group
Penguin Young Readers Group, 345 Hudson Street, New York, New York 10014, U.S.A.
Penguin Group (Canada), 90 Eglinton Avenue East, Suite 700, Toronto, Ontario, Canada M4P 2Y3
(a division of Pearson Penguin Canada Inc.)
Penguin Books Ltd, 80 Strand, London WC2R 0RL, England
Penguin Ireland, 25 St Stephen's Green, Dublin 2, Ireland (a division of Penguin Books Ltd)
Penguin Group (Australia), 250 Camberwell Road, Camberwell, Victoria 3124, Australia
(a division of Pearson Australia Group Pty Ltd)
Penguin Books India Pvt Ltd, 11 Community Centre, Panchsheel Park, New Delhi – 110 017, India
Penguin Group (NZ), 67 Apollo Drive, Rosedale, Auckland 0632, New Zealand
(a division of Pearson New Zealand Ltd)
Penguin Books (South Africa) (Pty) Ltd, 24 Sturdee Avenue, Rosebank, Johannesburg 2196, South Africa

First published in 1962 by Viking Penguin Inc.
Published simultaneously in Canada
Copyright © Ezra Jack Keats, 1962
All rights reserved
Library of Congress catalog number: 62-15441
ISBN 978-0-670-65400-0

Printed in the United States of America
Set in Bembo
85 87 89 90 88 86

To Tick, John, and Rosalie

6

One winter morning Peter woke up
and looked out the window. Snow
had fallen during the night. It cov-
ered everything as far as he could see.

After breakfast he put on his snowsuit and ran outside. The snow was piled up very high along the street to make a path for walking.

9

Crunch, crunch, crunch, his feet sank into the snow.

He walked with his toes pointing out, like this:

He walked with his toes
pointing in, like that:

Then he dragged his feet s–l–o–w–l–y
to make tracks.

And he found something sticking out
of the snow that made a new track.

It was a stick

— a stick that was just right for
smacking a snow-covered tree.

Down fell the snow —
plop!
— on top of Peter's head.

He thought it would be fun to join the big boys in their snowball fight, but he knew he wasn't old enough — not yet.

So he made a smiling snowman,

and he made angels.

He pretended
he was a mountain-climber.
He climbed up
a great big tall
heaping mountain of snow —

and slid all the way down.

He picked up a handful of snow — and another, and still another. He packed it round and firm and put the snowball in his pocket for tomorrow. Then he went into his warm house.

He told his mother all about his adventures
while she took off his wet socks.

And he thought and thought
and thought about them.

Before he got into bed he looked in his pocket.

His pocket was empty. The snowball wasn't there.

He felt very sad.

While he slept, he dreamed that the sun
had melted all the snow away.

But when he woke up his dream was gone.

The snow was still everywhere.

New snow was falling!

31

After breakfast he called to his friend from across the hall, and they went out together into the deep, deep snow.